*To Kelly
How's t...
Our Mother Cat has 5 babies*

NELL'S STORY OF LONG AGO

Helen Migan
Helen Migan

*To: Kelly
Dec 25, 1995
From: Nana
Helen Migan was Gigi's roommate in the hospital.*

Scythe Publications, Inc.
A Division of Winston-Derek Publishers Group, Inc.

© 1995 by Helen Migan

All rights reserved. No part of this book may be reproduced in any form without written permission from the publishers, except by a reviewer who may quote brief passages in a review to be printed in a newspaper or magazine.

First printing

PUBLISHED BY SCYTHE PUBLICATIONS, INC.
Nashville, Tennessee 37205

Library of Congress Catalog Card No: 92-84106
ISBN: 1-55523-593-X

Printed in the United States of America

Lovingly dedicated to the memory of my husband,
artist Louis Migan.

CONTENTS

1. New Experiences   1

2. A New Home   7

3. Sundays   11

4. Shut-In Days   15

5. Nell Learns About Babies   19

6. Tornado   23

7. Remembering and Forgetting   29

8. Autumn's Chill   33

9. Christmas Program   37

10. Tragedy   41

11. The New House   45

12. Night Alarm   51

13. A Happy Day   55

New Experiences

It was early in April and the sunshine was so inviting. Nell was enjoying the privilege of being outside alone. She had been told to stay in the yard and out of people's way. She felt so grown up, but she realized that her new freedom ended at the sidewalk. There were no other children in sight, but she was thrilled just to enjoy the cool fresh air. A sparrow or two lit on the sidewalk and appeared friendly. She watched them flit around and find a speck of food. Then they spread their tiny wings and flew away. There were no new leaves on the trees yet, so she had a good view of the brilliant cloudless sky. She was filled with wonder and content.

Finally from down the street Nell heard the steady clop-clop, clop-clop of horses feet coming her way. Their steps were slow and steady, for they were pulling a heavy dray. The driver shouted "Whoa!" The horses stopped almost in front of her. How exciting, she didn't even need to move!

The horses seemed glad to rest, for they nodded their heads and rattled their harnesses.

Two men jumped down from the dray and began to unload something big and heavy and black. As the men struggled to carry the heavy crate up the steps to the porch, Nell saw that their hands were very dirty. She supposed that they had been working around black sooty coal stoves. As she continued staring she saw how black their faces were too. *How strange?* she thought. *Don't their mothers make them wash with soap?*

She couldn't puzzle over this very long for activities along the street attracted her attention. The horses and the drivers moved on down the street with the dray.

Then Mama called from the house, "Come in now, Nell. Get washed and ready for lunch."

One morning, a few days later, Nell was awakened very early. After breakfast—which she hardly remembered because she was so sleepy—Mama shocked her wide awake. As she bustled busily about she said, "Come hurry and get washed. Then let me help you dress and comb your hair. You and I are going up north to visit Aunt Betsy. We will ride a long way on the train and we must be at the depot within an hour." Nell danced with excitement. She had never had a ride on a train, but she sensed Mama's happy concern and tried to stand still to be combed and dressed.

She looked very neat in her new shiny brown dress with a brown velvet neck band. (Before the day was over she found out that the bright shiny material was heavy and very scratchy inside.)

Within the hour Mama and Nell were sitting in the depot's huge waiting room. The sturdy benches were long, and uncomfortable seats were divided by strong iron arm rests. They were eagerly waiting for the train.

There wasn't much to see looking straight ahead so Nell got on her knees to peek over the slatted back of the bench. To her amazement she saw two nicely dressed ladies with feather-plumed hats facing her. They seemed to be chatting pleasantly. She was surprised to see that their faces were very black!

Mama said to Nell "You had better turn around and sit down." Nell didn't need to be told twice! Her eyes were wide with wonder, but she felt comfortable sitting quietly by Mama.

At last they heard the long shrill blast of the whistle of the coming train. Then the chugging and hissing as the big black engine came to a stop. The shiny brass bell on top of the engine swinging its ding, ding, ding. It seemed to say "Hurry, hurry".

The conductor in a splendid blue uniform called in a loud voice, "All abooaarrd!" as he placed a low metal step on the brick pavement for people to step up to the high steps of the train. Then he boosted Nell all the way up to the platform of the coach where Mama joined her.

They entered the door and saw the long coach lined with seats on both sides of a narrow aisle. The cushioned seats were covered with beautiful green upholstery. Nell thought that everything was very pretty. She chose to sit next to the window. After two short blasts of the engine's whistle, the train started to move. Very slowly at first, then faster and faster till Nell was almost dizzy. Soon they were leaving the busy streets with lines of houses behind. They were out in open country where every house seemed to have fields for yards and barns of many sizes.

Then she started watching the tall poles whiz by and was soon napping. When she woke up the poles were still close by but also lots of trees and woods.

She wanted a drink, so Mama took her to the water cooler at the other end of the coach. She had a hard time trying to walk because the coach at high speed was rocking sideways. She had to hang on to Mama's hand tightly, and Mama had to catch hold of the back of seats as she went along.

Arriving back at her own seat, Nell decided that trying to walk on a swaying coach was fun, so she decided that she wanted another drink. But Mama said no for now.

She sat quietly for a few minutes then she whispered to Mama, "I need to go to the toilet."

So she got a chance to go down that rocking aisle again. But Mama didn't seem to enjoy the fun. The door to the toilet was right next to the water cooler, but the latch was way up high. Mama could easily reach it, so she went in with Nell. What a surprise awaited Nell! This toilet had no bottom and when she looked down at the ground, the gravel and railroad ties were whizzing along backward beneath them. How frightening! She was glad that Mama was there to hold her. She was very glad to get back safely to her seat. Since she had been awakened very early that morning she couldn't keep her eyes open any longer.

When the train started to slow down she opened her eyes and Mama said, "Here we're at Hometown now and must get off. See out the window, there is Uncle Frank on the pavement waiting for us."

They hurriedly got their belongings together and were helped down the steps by the smiling conductor.

From the train window Uncle Frank looked very short, but as Nell looked up at him from her short height he seemed quite tall.

Uncle Frank shook hands with Mama. Looking at Nell who could not make out his smile which was almost hidden by his short sandy moustache, he asked "How did you like your train ride? Now you'll get a chance to stretch your legs. My rig is just across the street. Come along let's go." He took her by the hand and started across the dusty, unpaved street. He carried Mama's suitcase in his other hand.

When they reached the rig, Nell found that is was a topless two seated buggy but was most delighted to see the two brown horses hitched to it.

Uncle Frank lifted her high into the front seat then helped Mama up to sit beside her. He went around and untied the horses, climbed up the other side of the buggy and took up the reins. The horses were so patient and obedient but knew they were headed home, so they needed no special urging or guiding.

Soon they were leaving Hometown behind. The unpaved street and the dusty road were very much alike, only the country road was barely one track wide. When the open fields were shut off by roadside bushes, Nell had nothing to watch but the backs of the horses and the buggy wheels turning in the loose sand. The sand would follow the wheel upward a few inches only to fall back in the rut. She watched, hoping the sand could follow the wheel higher. It kept rising then falling, rising then falling back endlessly. Tiring of that, Nell noticed the chiming sound of the four tug chains. As she listened she could hear a sort of music in the incessant jingle-jingle which was very pleasant.

Presently Uncle Frank said, "We are coming to the old Grist Mill where we get our wheat ground into flour, and you will see a lot of water." Nell perked up.

Then Mama said, "As the water falls over the dam it turns the mill wheel as it is needed. After it flows over the dam it rushes under the bridge and we will ride right over it. It is very pretty."

Nell was all eyes and ears at the sound and sight of the tumbling water. She had never seen anything like that in her whole life. (In later years when visiting the mighty Niagara, she was impressed and thrilled, but she didn't feel the awe and astonishment as with this unexpected sight!)

Uncle Frank turned to her and said, "What did you think of that?"

Nell's answer was quick and unexpected, "Well! I guess there is enough water to wash your feet."

She had something new to think about for a long ways. There was nothing pretty or exciting for a weary little girl. Only the road, the horses, the bushes on both sides of the road. She leaned against Mama and napped the rest of the way.

She partly awakened and realized that they were at Aunt Betsy's house. After a very good supper which she hardly remembered, Nell was gently helped out of her scratchy clothes into her nightie and tucked into the big bed. Mama would share the big bed with her later. Nell was sound asleep when patient Mama cuddled in beside her.

She dreamed about the train ride or perhaps the beautiful Waterfall.

A New Home

A FEW DAYS HAD PASSED since Mama and Nell had arrived at Aunt Betsy's. Nell had been happily exploring the yard. Here was lots of room for just running freely here and there.

Her favorite pastime was watching a mother hen with her brood of tiny chicks. Some were white, some brown, and some were black and white. They looked like balls of fluff running around on tiny toothpick legs. She must not try to pick one up because mother hen was apt to fly right in her face.

Aunt Betsy said, "Just sit on the step and watch how the mother hen helps them find food and talks to them. She says, 'Cluck, cluck' softly. They answer with 'Peep, peep' or 'cheep, cheep.' What funny chicken talk! See how cunning they are when they try to scratch as their mother does to find food! You can help me when I bring them some water and grain."

In the meantime Mama had left shortly after breakfast to walk a short way up the hill to The House. She was trying to clean it because it hadn't been lived in for quite awhile. The house was sided with weather-beaten gray shingles. Inside it had four rooms. Two rooms downstairs and two rooms upstairs, tight under the slanting roof. Underneath this small house was an old dirt floored cellar. You could go down through inside stairs or the outside stairs. These outside stairs were covered with slanted double doors which kept the rain out. When these heavy doors were open, the men would carry heavy bushels of potatoes, rutabagas or apples from the loaded wagon directly to the cellar bins without going through the house.

Mama was busy in the kitchen. Since the walls were made of rough unpainted boards, she decided to paper them with clean newspapers. She used carpet tacks carefully protected by small squares of cardboard. She tacked each corner then she slid the next sheet against it. Soon the kitchen looked clean and bright. Not all the print was right side up!

When the freight train brought the furniture to Hometown, Uncle Frank loaned his team, wagon and driver to go to town and fetch it. Of course Papa went along to help load. They made more than one trip.

With all the commotion of unloading and arranging furniture, setting up the black wood-burning stove and so forth, Nell still stayed contentedly with Aunt Betsy.

In a day or so, Mama had a stove to cook on. The pump was just outside the west door, so she had water to cook with and also to heat for washing dishes.

Then the family, Mama, Papa, two brothers and Nell moved in! Alan and Danny were bursting with excitement. They were eager to tell how much they loved the country. There was so much to see and do! Alan could actually help in the fields. Danny tagged along. Since he proved himself useful, Aunt Betsy called on him for many armfuls of wood and buckets of water. He could gather eggs in the afternoon. It was fun to hunt for the eggs in the nests the hens had hidden in the haymow or strawstacks. He was rewarded with one of Aunt Betsy's sugar cookies with one raisin in the center. But now at the table he had to be reminded not to talk with his mouth full.

Alan was older and more serious. He was looking for opportunities to be helpful, so that he could begin to earn money. Their cousins were nearer his age, Cliff and Lloyd were also pleased to have nearby pals. Though they were eager to teach the "city kids" a few tricks, they didn't pull any mean tricks. Alan soon learned to use the simple tools with ease; hay forks, shovels, and hoes. He learned to milk cows by hand and do chores around farm animals. Soon he was asked for by the neighbors who needed extra help. He became quite busy at neighboring farms and was pleased to be earning money.

Nell was never lacking for attention. At the table Papa prepared her plate. Since she was running about outside all day she was ready to eat. She ate quietly listening to everything everybody said. Besides, she had Mama all to herself most of the day. It was exciting to listen to Papa and the boys tell about their work and a lot of interesting things.

One sunny warm day, Mama said, "It is so nice out. I think you could be outside alone if we can find a place without tall grass or thistles." By now Nell was used to being barefoot, but thistles were too picky for hands and arms as well as feet. Nell clapped her hands and said, "Goody, goody." Mama went out the back door to find a suitable dry place where Nell could play. It had to be near the open door where Mama could keep an eye on her. The woods were close by on this side of the house. The grass and weeds were too thick and high everywhere else. For a little girl to play contentedly alone it was a problem. Mama looked at the chip pile. It was near the wood pile. Also it was nice and dry. By leaving the door open, Mama could hear her and see her. Mama's knowledge of mosquitoes and snakes she kept to herself so Nell was never afraid.

Mama said, "Bring out your little iron horse and green wagon and you can haul chips to your lumber yard."

Nell was delighted. Now she knew what horses and wagons were used for and she could talk real horse talk: "Giddap, giddap, whoa!" that horses understood.

Mama continued in the house with her unpacking. She decided to begin with her fancy dishes which she had carefully wrapped and packed in crumpled newspaper. A little later, beginning to tire of her play, Nell ran to the house but stopped short at the door. What was the matter with Mama? There was crumpled newspaper all over the floor, a few nice dishes were stacked on the table. But Mama was crying! Nell wanted to cry too. She couldn't remember ever having seen her Mama crying before. She ran to Mama's side and said, "Mama, why are you crying?"

Mama tried to wipe her tears with her apron as she took Nell on her lap. She tried in a choked voice to explain. "Those train people must have thrown these boxes around or dropped them, for many of my prettiest dishes are broken or cracked. There are cups without handles, pitchers without spouts, plates broken beyond use. O dear, and I had wrapped them so carefully in all this newspaper."

Nell's spirits rose as with two cracked dishes she returned to the play happily, forgetting what she had gone to the house for.

After a while she got an idea. "Maybe there will be some more dishes that I can have." Back to the house she went.

Sure enough, Mama still teary-eyed was holding a beautiful cake plate painted with pink roses in her hand. How Nell wished that it could be hers. She waited breathlessly as Mama looked it over carefully. Mama swallowed and said, "Thank goodness, this was a present from Alan and it's all right." Nell's hopes fell. Then Mama went on, "Over there are some cups and saucers you can have." Smiles spread over Nell's face as she gathered the pretty pieces. She was pleased but puzzled. She was so sorry that Mama was sad. How could Nell be so happy? Was Nell selfish?

Sundays

NELL AWAKENED TO ANOTHER HOT DAY. Since she had lived in this house a short time she had been allowed to go barefoot. Her feet were not so tender now and she was enjoying the freedom of running in the soft grass. But this morning Mama said "While you are nice and clean after last night's bath, put on your clean stockings and shoes before you run around."

Nell puzzled, "Why?"

"Because we are going to Sunday School. Today is Sunday," answered Mama.

"What is Sunday School?" asked Nell.

Mama answered, "It is a place where folks go to study the Bible and learn about God. There is no Church near us, so we meet in the schoolhouse. There will be other boys and girls there and the grown-ups."

"Where is the schoolhouse? How do we get there?" Nell's questions were coming fast for she was getting excited to see what this was all about. Mama said, "We will walk. It isn't that far. It's just over the hill beyond Lily and Jane's house."

Nell put on her shoes and long black stockings. Papa was already dressed in white shirt and tie. Mama put on a big hat, and since it was such a hot day she didn't wear a coat over her pretty white shirtwaist.

The three started out looking fresh and tidy. Before they arrived at the schoolhouse, their shoes and Mama's black skirt were covered with dust. There were quite a few neighbors already gathered. Some had come longer distances in buggies or wagons and tied their horses to the fence posts.

When Nell saw all those strangers, she became very shy and hung tightly to Papa's hand. Papa proudly introduced her as his little girl. But she couldn't see any children. All she could see were the tall legs with black trousers. She felt as if she was in a forest of black trees, only these moved around.

Finally, when the grown-ups got seated at the larger desks, she noticed some bearded faces. The meeting began with singing. Nell liked that. Some of the songs she had heard Mama and Papa sing, *Jesus, Lover of My Soul* and *In the Sweet By and By*.

Then a man with a long black coat got up to talk. Nell thought he was handsome with his beard. He was friendly and smiling. Nell soon lost interest, and began to look around. Then she began to feel hungry. After a long time they sang more songs. Then there were different men saying long prayers. Nell was glad that Papa only prayed a short blessing before meals.

There was a brief pause then Sunday School began. They gathered in small groups in different parts of the school room. Aunt Betsy was Nell's teacher. Nell was pleased and felt comfortable in her class of small people.

Aunt Betsy had a small picture card. She read the story of Elijah. The Bible said that there had been a very dry season and God told Elijah to go down to the brook to stay where he could have water to drink and food would be sent to him. The picture showed Elijah dressed in a long robe waiting while a bird called a raven flew toward him with a round sandwich in its beak. Nell was sure it was a delicious beef sandwich. She was so hungry. She could almost taste how delicious it was. Aunt Betsy said Elijah obeyed God and God kept his promise. Nell always liked the story of Elijah.

Everybody stood around after dismissal and visited. They agreed to meet next Sunday. After the long dusty walk home Nell's appetite did justice to Mama's good dinner.

Shut-In Days

No matter what the weather, rainy, snowy or windy, Mama was always busy. Bread to bake, clothes to wash on the scrub board, ironing and mending torn clothes or darning the family's socks took many tedious hours. Mama made use of every minute.

Nell was left to herself. She often got bored and wished Mama could pay attention to her. In the kitchen she was surrounded by the gigantic puzzle of newspapered walls. She knew that Mama had the key to this great mystery. So while Mama was kneading bread dough Nell would point to a big black squiggle and ask, "What does this say?"

Mama answered, "*T*."

Nell went on to the next, "What is this?"

Mama: "*H*."

Nell persisted, "This?"

Mama patiently: "*E. T H E* spells *the*."

Nell waited a minute, "That doesn't make sense."

But Mama said, "See if you can find another word, *the*." And the game of hunt and find began. When Nell tired of it she looked around for something else to do.

Nearly every day, she returned to the puzzle on the wall. She tackled the biggest print she could reach. Then the questions to

Mama began all over, "What is this letter, Mama?" Finally, light began to dawn when she found that *The Hometown Journal* was a name for the newspaper. The thrills began to grow as she tackled the little boxed figure stories, *Elmer Fudd, George Bungle, Krazy Kat*. Nell could read. What a joy! But reading material was scarce. *The Michigan Farmer* was the weekly magazine; a small Sunday School tract or the Bible verse card were almost the only current printed things that came her way.

Mama had taught her all the familiar nursery rhymes from her bountiful store. She also sang familiar hymns and folk songs from her reliable memory. There was no printed Nursery Rhyme book in Nell's childhood. The family library consisted of The Holy Bible (in daily use), a hymn book without music, and a moderate sized box of books that was left packed. Nell discovered it much later on.

But that fall Aunt Bea came for a visit. She was such a gentle, smiley person. Since there were no spare bedrooms, Nell got the chance to share her bed with Aunt Bea. What a comfort to snuggle close to Aunt Bea's flannel softness.

In the morning the air was quite frosty, so Aunt Bea and Nell lingered in bed while Mama stoked the kitchen stove preparing a hot breakfast.

Aunt Bea began reciting nursery rhymes and Nell happily joined in with the ones she knew, *Jack and Jill Went Up the Hill* or *The House that Jack Built*. Then Aunt Bea taught Nell some new ones.

> "There was a crow
> Sat in the snow,
> As black as any ink.
> He gave a squawk
> And off he walked,
> To Mexico, I think."

"Hi diddledy, dump
A rabbit hid in a stump.
The doggie can't find him, you know
He traveled all day
From his home far away
Through the very deep cold snow
But the rabbit kept snug
Like a bug in a rug
And laughed at the old dog in his sleeve
When the night fell
The doggie said, 'Well
I'd better take my leave.'"

Nell Learns About Babies

ANOTHER DAY TWO LITTLE COUSINS, just about Nell's size came down to play. Their names were Lily and Jane. They were nice and browned from being outside every day in the sun. They were also barefooted. When they went outside, they said, "Let's go to the barn." Nell followed but her feet were too tender and her short legs couldn't run very fast. She called. "Girls, Wait!" The girls just laughed. They managed to get the heavy barn door open and went inside the barn to explore. Nell didn't like the dark barn so she stood at the door and looked. When they came out, they still couldn't think of anything to play except to race and squeal and chase each other at which Nell was too slow. As she tried to tag along she continued to call, "Wait, girls, Wait!"

Some days after that Nell and Mama went up to visit the cousins. To Nell's surprise there were two other small children, a boy and a tiny baby. There were no toys. When Lily and Jane asked her to go outside to play, Nell was not yet ready to leave the fascinating baby.

After they got home, Nell kept talking about that sweet baby. Finally she asked, "Mama, can't we get a baby?" Mama said she was much too busy. Nell didn't give up. She kept it in her mind.

When the *Big Wish Book* from Chicago came in later summer Nell spent many quiet hours avidly turning pages and wondering about the pictures. The dollar signs had no meaning for her. As she looked at the pretty women in all kinds of different dresses, pretty hats and underwear she was not too impressed. Finally, wonder of wonders, there were pages of *babies*. They looked so real. This was the answer to her dearest wish.

She ran excitedly calling, "Mama, Mama! Here is where we can get a baby. Look, just look! I've already picked one out. Will you send for this one? Isn't she sweet?"

Jumping up and down she continued pleading. Mama had a hard time explaining that these were not real babies. Only the clothes were for sale.

What a disappointment! She lost interest for the time being in the Wish Book.

One day the cousins on the hill came along on their way to the huckleberry patch. Lily and Jane had to help pick the small berries but their mother was pushing the baby buggy through the sand. It was difficult going. They stopped at Nell's house. Mama said, "Leave the baby with us. Nell will love to help take care of her." Nell was delighted.

When the buggy was brought into the house it was easy to push back and forth on the smooth kitchen floor. Baby Louella was sweet and endearing as her mother rested a few minutes and nursed her.

Nell completely ignored Lily and Jane since her attention was on the baby. Mama said, "Just don't worry—with the baby in the buggy, Nell can push if she cries. But since she has just been fed, she will probably go to sleep."

The berry pickers took off with their jangling pails.

Nell was so happy. She was big enough to have such an important job. She didn't think she could wait for the baby to cry. She didn't have to wait long. Soon a shrill wail, "Waa! Waaa-aaa" came from the buggy. Nell flew into action; she pushed the buggy across the kitchen, then backed up the other way. She wasn't big enough to turn the buggy around. So back and forth, she went. "Waa, Waaa," continued to the ears.

Mama said, "Try singing to her." So Nell tried *Old Black Joe* and other choruses, but nothing worked; Baby Louella was not sleepy. Mama was enjoying Nell's discomfort and decided to let Nell find out that babies have needs that take lots of patience. When Mama thought that Baby Louella was getting over exercised she picked her up and comforted her. She knew that picking wild huckleberries was tedious and time consuming. Probably the berry pickers wouldn't be back at least for two hours.

When Baby Louella went to sleep and was back in her buggy, Nell was content to leave well enough alone. She went quietly outside to play.

Mother didn't hear any more from Nell, "Why don't we get a baby?"

Tornado

The hot July sun was having full possession of the beautiful blue sky. But the air was so muggy and hot it was hard to breathe.

Mama said, "We are going to get a storm out of this," as she cleared the noon lunch dishes away.

Papa said, "I am going to take the scythe and cut some marsh grass down in the swale. Marsh grass makes a good cover over a shelter for the animals until I can build a better shed."

Mama said, "The swale isn't far from the house. I can take little Nell along so both of us can get out of this stuffy house. Maybe we can find some shade for her."

Papa went on ahead and started swinging the sharp scythe through the deep tall grass. Skillfully he lay the mown grass in even flat rows behind him.

As Mama and Nell came along, Mama explained, "I don't think the mosquitoes will bother us too much in this bright sunshine. They like the darkening summer evenings to come out to pester us. But you must be careful where you step or sit for there are moss covered logs and stumps to trip you. Leave the wild flowers alone, and especially don't pull on the grass for this marsh grass has sharp edges that cut little fingers and bare legs."

When they got near Papa, he already had quite a bit cut. Then he trampled down a patch of wild grass and told Nell to stay within that area.

But it was so very hot in the sunshine. There was no shade. The taller bushes and trees were beyond the marsh. They shut off any little breeze that might have come drifting by. Nell was so hot and tired. She wanted a drink of water. She was so thirsty. When would Papa get through? Mama was busy with that big hayfork piling the cut grass. She wasn't paying attention to Nell.

Nell was beginning to fidget and absentmindedly touched the grass running the edge across her finger. She howled in pain and the sight of blood running across her hand made her scream louder, "Mama, Mama!"

Mama came as fast as she could and saw that a fairly small cut had been the cause of all that crying and quantity of blood. "But Nell, I warned you about that grass." She wiped away the blood with the edge of her apron. "Now, there, there," she said soothingly, "just wait a little longer for I want to help Papa. I know how hot it is, but when we go back to the house I'll take care of your finger."

So Nell settled down in the hot wilted grass and mourned her discomfort. It seemed that finger began to hurt worse. She was feeling sorry for herself. There was still nothing to play with, nothing to do. *How much longer,* she wondered, *are they going to stay?*

Finally she began whimpering, "I'm so thirsty. I want a drink of water."

Mama looked at the darkening sky. It looked threatening to her, so she said to Papa in a calm voice, "It looks like we are going to get a rain storm. I'll take Nell and go back to the house. I'll put in the upstairs windows. The sky is getting blacker. You had better come along too."

Nell didn't need to be coaxed to start, she was already picking her way over the tramped down grass that led the way out.

As Mama and Nell hurried along a few big drops of rain began to come down. Nearing the house they ran to get inside, just as pelting hailstones covered the ground white.

Mama thought of the open outside cellar door and said to Nell, "You wait here in the kitchen while I run down to close the cellar door."

Nell was so scared she forgot about her cut finger. She went to the top steps and looked to see Mama struggling to shut the heavy doors against a cascade of water coming in down the cellar steps. Her screams took over again. Thunder and lightning added to her terror.

When Mama returned to the kitchen to start upstairs, Nell could not let her out of sight. She clung to Mama's drenched skirts and was pulled up the stairs. Mama had to put in a south window, then one in the north room. And though the lightning and thunder was more frightening, Nell felt comforted by Mama's calm manner of thinking.

Barely had Mama and Nell got back down the steps when there came a loud knocking, pounding on the rough boarded door.

When Mama got the door open a scared, soaked-through neighbor's boy shouted, "Get your shawl and come; Abbot's barn has blown down! Little Eileen Farr was in the barn under all the hay. Go to Mrs. Farr; she is very anxious." Then he ran on.

Mama put on her brown shawl over her head, tucked a bundle of towels and bandages under her arm. Then she took Nell by the hand and both stepped out into the storm. When they got to the road they could see the low ground where rapidly swirling water started to cross the road. She explained to Nell calmly that she must go down the road to Aunt Betsy's even though she had to wade through water. By this time they could see Aunt Betsy out on the porch waving for Nell to come. Then Mama started up the hill to Mrs. Farr's.

By this time Nell's terror took another turn; not only was Mama going the other way, but the water was getting deeper. It came to her knees and then her waist and nearly to her armpits. Soon she reached firmer ground and she was near Auntie's comforting arms. When her wails subsided she enjoyed her stay with Aunt Betsy.

Meanwhile Papa had gone ahead to Abbots where he found many neighbors gathered at the disaster. Little Eileen had been found alive under the heavy beam of an old fashioned horse drawn hay baler. The heavy beam had held up tons of hay above her. She was badly hurt and unconscious as they carried her across the road and back up the road to her frightened mother.

A neighbor rode horseback hurriedly for the doctor about eleven miles away. So it would be late at night before the doctor could get to the little girl.

Eileen had been with her older brother Earl to watch the Abbots put a huge load of hay in the haymow. It was fascinating to see the extra horses pull the slings which were arranged in layers as the hay was loaded on the wagon by means of pulleys and ropes. They lifted large bundles high in the barn and dropped it into the haymow. Men were hurrying because they had seen and heard the clouds and thunder. Earl said, "Eileen, we had better hurry home. It's going to rain."

They started but when they got to the huge barn door, Eileen was frightened and turned back. Earl couldn't coax her and she was too big for him to carry. By the time they had turned back the storm struck; Earl didn't know what happened to Eileen. The barn was flattened; all the animals were scattered with fright. The men drove the harnessed horses right over the leveled shingled roof of the barn.

The gathered men helped surround the frightened animals, but when Earl told them that Eileen ran back into the barn, they all began searching for her. After finding her and getting her there was nothing to do but wait.

When the doctor arrived after dark, he found her much battered and bruised but no broken bones. He remained the rest of the night and when she regained consciousness he said she would be ill a long time. And also that she could not be active as before.

Nell was allowed to visit Eileen a couple of times. By the time Nell was old enough to go to school, the Farrs had moved away.

Nell never forgot that terrific storm. Many times she recalled her fear and terror during that devastating Tornado!

It's no wonder she forgot all about her sore cut finger.

Remembering and Forgetting

Late summer days seemed quite the same day after day, so Nell found herself with nothing fun to do. The different playhouses that she had busied herself with in the long summer days were being left pretty much alone.

The one in the corncrib, which had an exciting upstairs, was needed to store 'the new crop' of eared corn. The dolls and doll dishes were taken back into the house.

The playhouse in the fish shanty was not very suitable in the first place. It had no window. The only light came through the open door. Besides it sat in the open sunshine and the hot summer sun turned it into a sweltering bake oven. Also, it was covered with black tar paper which when heated by the sun smelled strongly of melting tar. Its use soon passed when the novelty of occupation wore off. As soon as the great threshing machine pulled in, eviction was at hand. The fish shanty was needed as a storage bin for oats!

Nell spent more time now daydreaming. The great outdoors was not quite so inviting. The one or two books she had were looked at many times. *The Michigan Farmer* was welcomed in the mail and the once a month *Good Stories* which Mama read eagerly. (A year's subscription to it cost twenty five cents.) One such paper carried the story of *Uncle Wiggily and Nurse Jane*, the muskrat lady housekeeper. Nell was thrilled and could hardly wait for the next episode.

But it was such a long time between new stories that she idled away time with empty dreams. Then one day she got an idea that prompted action.

The baby chicks that she had tended so faithfully were now all feathered out. Some of them looked like their mother, Baldy.

Baldy had been Nell's favorite mother hen since early Spring. Her smooth silvery gray feathers were so neat. Her head was fitted with a snowy lacy cap. She looked like a grand lady. She was so proud and protective of her babies. Nell wondered if Mama would give Baldy to her for her very own.

She thought, *Alan and Danny each have a young calf to call their own. Papa has the horses and cows. Mama has Jack and Jack has Mama. The cats belong to the family and I have nothing of my own.*

At the breakfast table, Nell watched her chance to get into the conversation. Getting up courage she burst out, "Mama, will you give me Baldy and her brood for my very own? I think she knows me and is very gentle."

Mama flashed a quick glance at Papa. Nell knew what was coming next. No important decisions were made in this family until Papa and Mama were in full agreement. Papa looked at Nell and said, "Well, I guess Nell is getting big enough to have chickens of her own." Then he added, "And the food in summer is not a great expense." (Nell hadn't thought of that.)

But, she promised, "I will be sure to fasten them in every night." She knew that faithful Jack would watch the yard all night and would bark at any enemy prowlers such as weasels, skunks, or rats and frighten them away.

Ownership gave Nell a new sense of importance and pride. The days seemed more promising. Nell didn't realize that she was living in the "backwoods." She didn't feel that she was missing anything. She could keep busy. She was happy. Life was great!

Everything continued smoothly for a few days. One morning Papa said, "Nell, how do you like Cherry's new calf Beauty? Isn't she a fine lovable little animal? Would you like to trade Baldy and her brood for Beauty, the calf? You can feed Beauty her milk for she drinks from a pail now."

Nell's brain went into high gear. *Beauty is a loving pet. Papa won't have any use for Baldy, and she will still be here with the other chickens. So I can have both Baldy and Beauty.* This seemed like a good deal.

Nell eagerly said yes.

Papa said, "You want to be sure, for a bargain is a bargain; once you agree to a deal it is for good."

Nell quickly responded, "I'm sure. I'll like Beauty."

She felt sure she had nothing to worry about. But she missed the disapproving look that Mama gave Papa.

Day followed day and nothing much was happening. The mornings were quite chilly now. Nell stayed in bed a little longer then came to the breakfast table sleepy-eyed. But she was jolted wide awake when Papa said, "I think we will have to sell some chickens because the oat crop wasn't too good this year. I don't want to have the horses without their oats this winter. Mrs. Bowman over on Lake Road wants to start with a flock of chickens so she can have fresh eggs on hand. I think I'll let her have Baldy and her brood to get started."

He glanced at Nell out of the corner of his eye. She missed the twinkle and instantly took the bait, "Oh please, Papa, don't let her have Baldy. I still love her," and she burst into tears.

Papa said, "I thought we had a bargain; didn't you promise? I thought you liked Beauty."

Nell was miserable, but she knew better than to continue to plead. Now she realized what making an easy promise meant. She waited till Papa solemnly left the house for the field. The she ran meekly to Mama to ask, "What can I do to get Baldy back? I didn't know that Papa would sell her." Her eyes filled with tears and her chin quivered.

Mama said, "Remember how eager you were to receive something easily. You did not think that a promise given is meant to be kept. Another time take a moment to think and don't rush into such a deal."

"Oh Mama, I'll be real careful. Please talk to Papa and tell him how much I want Baldy back."

Mama said, "I'll talk to Papa and tell him that you didn't mean to back out of your promise. That you intend to be more thoughtful and cautious."

Nell kept close watch for Papa's return to the house, but she didn't run to greet him happily as she usually did. She kept quiet and was subdued at the noontime lunch, while Mama tactfully presented Nell's case. More or less Mama assured Papa that Nell was a much wiser little girl. "I think Nell will think carefully in the future. She is very sorry and could be happy again if Papa could forget the bad bargain and accept a kiss instead."

Papa cleared his throat, straightened in his chair, smiled and opened his arms as Nell gleefully ran into them. "How about helping me fix fence this afternoon if Mama can spare you?"

The screen door banged behind the three of them as they went merrily off.

Faithful Jack was not far behind.

Autumn's Chill

WARM SUNNY DAYS PASSED SWIFTLY AWAY. The harvest of field and garden was almost over. Fall had come. Nell could no longer freely run barefoot outside. The clouds were gray and threatening. The wind was brisk and chilly. So Nell was content to stay inside for the time being. Her summer tan was fading fast. Mama noticed that Nell seemed listless and not her usual lively self. Mama asked, "What's the matter? Do you feel sick?"

Nell shook her head, no.

When Mama asked the friendly family doctor, Nielson, he said, "Dress her warmly and send her outside every day, except if it's raining, of course."

Mama ripped up an old, wool overcoat and made Nell a bulky but very warm petticoat. Then with her knitted woolen stockings Nell was well protected from the cold.

Outside she went to run and chase with watchful Black Jack. He was a great pal.

The ground was not yet frozen, so Papa was doing the fall plowing with the horses, Jim and Maude.

After the noon meal, with the horses having munched their hay, Papa was ready to start back to the field. Nell and Jack were ready, too. Jack would bark and bounce ahead but Nell, bundled till she looked like a pumpkin with legs, followed behind.

Maude had to walk in the last turned furrow, while Jim walked up on the unplowed sod. As the plow turned the rolling mass of sod to the right, a new flat bottomed furrow was made. This was where Papa walked, holding fast to the long plow handles to keep the plow straight. To guide the horses he had the long reins looped behind his back; their ends trailed the furrow behind Papa. That was where Nell took her place. She took up the ends of the reins and pretending to drive the team, she would call out, "Giddap, Gee, Eeeasy now, Whoa!" The horses only minded Papa.

Back and forth across the long field they went, back and forth all afternoon. The horses, first pulling the heavy plow then Papa trying to hold the plow steady, but often he was snapped sideways when the plow hit a snag or a stone in the way. Last of all tagged Nell. Sometimes she would sit at the end of the field while Papa and the team made a complete round.

When Jack tired of sniffing for rabbits, or frogs, or chasing butterflies, he lay snoozing on a sunny patch of grass, patiently waiting, waiting.

In the late afternoon the horses began to hesitate at the end of the field nearest the barn. They would look toward the barn, prick up their ears (only to go on when Papa clicked with his lips "ck, ck"). They knew that they were ready for a drink and supper of hay and oats. At last, Papa said, "Whoa!" He unhitched the team and left the plow where it stood. Then he lifted tired Nell onto Jim's broad back. She held tight onto the shiny harness and was thrilled to have a ride back to the house and a warm supper.

Soon the days began to grow colder. Thanksgiving Day would soon be here. The next exciting time was butchering time. Nell was kept in the house and not allowed to watch out the window. But soon the activity moved into the house, and the one porker was skewered and hung on the tripod 'gin pole' away from cats and dogs. The scrubbed, snowy whiteness of the skin held promises, the winter's supply of delicacies to come. The first taste would be fresh liver for supper, fried and tender. The heart and tongue would be ground up or pickled. The sweetbreads were used with hash brown potatoes for breakfast.

Then Mama made sausage. She ground the fresh lean meat with a mixture of spices that really made one hungry at the first whiff of the delicious smells. She froze long bags stuffed with the raw product. Also she lightly fried some patties, packed them in deep crocks, covered them with the freshly rendered lard and they could keep to be used in summer.

Best of all was the treat of roast spare ribs for Thanksgiving dinner. Only the ribs were not 'spare' and the long bone was not cut either. The whole length ribs were put in the big roaster with all the meat on them. With sage dressing it was a feast to be remembered. Baked spare ribs, mashed potatoes, gravy, baked beans, baked squash, pickles, and spicy pumpkin pie with slathers of real whipped cream filled the laden table.

After Papa asked the blessing, each one ate his fill and felt truly thankful for many blessings.

CHRISTMAS PROGRAM

REMEMBERING THANKSGIVING WAS SOON LAID ASIDE as the brothers began to talk about Christmas.

"Nell, you had better be extra good because Santa Claus is watching you. He will be coming with his reindeer and sleigh to only good girls," said Alan.

Danny reminded her, "Be sure to mind your manners. Santa wants to hear you say 'please' and 'thank you.'" In the meantime they both began to tease and say, "You must go to bed early if you expect to find goodies in your stocking Christmas morning."

Nell became more curious and excited. It seemed that Christmas was coming soon, but there was nothing for her to do.

On the sly Mama had been doing some shopping in the big Wish Book. Also, she kept the sewing machine busy. In the evenings, by the dim kerosene lamplight, her knitting needles kept up a steady 'click, click, click.' She was quietly planning and making gifts of mittens, scarves, hoods, and wristlets. She was limited by the colors of her yarn mostly black or dark blue; the red she used sparingly.

The boys kept up a steady chatter about the Christmas program at school. In rural schools, in those days, the teacher's rating depended not a little on the success of the annual Christmas program.

So the supper table conversation was filled with the excitement of the coming program. Danny was going to recite *'Twas the Night Before Christmas*. He was studying and rehearsing night after night. Nell was getting it pretty well memorized also. He had a secret delight in the daring lines, "He had a broad face and little round belly that shook when he laughed like a bowl full of jelly." He spoke them very distinctly and with courage. Nell was now completely involved in the coming unknown program Friday night. December was true to its seasonal offering of deep snow, cold frosty nights, and brilliant starlit skies. Daylight ended early, so it was already dark when the family was bundled and wedged in the narrow sleighbox to start for the schoolhouse. Jim and Maude were eager to get some exercise after being fast in their stalls for days. The sleigh runners squeaked over the frosted track, and how the bells tinkled a merry tune as the horses kept up a brisk trot in the cold.

Nell's excitement grew as she saw the dimly lit windows. While Papa tied and blanketed the horses, her fears began to take over. She was quiet when Alan carried her in over the deep snow. But her eyes widened in surprise and wonder as she saw the immense tree in the front corner of the room. It was so beautifully decorated with strings of popcorn, popcorn balls and apples, colored tissue, paper chains, cut out stars and chains of paper dolls holding hands. Too pretty to try to see everything! The room was so crowded Nell found herself sitting by Lily and Jane in the small seats for little kids. They chatted and had a merry time. The cousins had parts in the program and took their turn.

Their brother, only six, said a traditional poem that nearly brought down the house. He was very brave and spoke clearly:

"Ole St. Nick is short and thick
So I've been told by Ma.
But I've seen him, he's tall and slim
He looks just like my Pa."

All the school sang several songs. Nell knew *Jingle Bells* and *Silent Night*. The program came to an end.

But the excitement grew because every one was talking about Santa coming. Lily and Jane could hardly contain themselves. Then they heard loud thumps in the hall. Nell looked around for Papa. He was way on the other side of the room.

Then there was a jingle of sleigh bells! The door opened. A masked figure in a long brown fur coat came in shouting "Ho! Ho! Merry Christmas!" Nell made a dive under the desks and huddled against the wall. Lily and Jane coaxed, "Come out. Santa has a big sack of peanuts and candy." Nell was still afraid, but since the girls were eagerly watching for their treat, she finally peeked out. It was very noisy, but everyone seemed to be enjoying themselves so she waited and was filled with wonder. At last someone handed her a plump bag and she was very happy. Also she was happy that Santa was kept busy with others and stayed at a distance from her. Getting in the sleigh, snuggling in the smelly horse blankets, riding home was uneventful. She was too sleepy to talk but she had a wonderful time! When Aunt Bea went back to her home, Nell was sad. She missed Aunt Bea so much.

At Christmas time Santa Claus brought Nell a handmade cloth doll with a China head beautifully dressed.

Years later Nell discovered who Santa's helper was.

Tragedy

THE CHRISTMAS PROGRAM had been a neighborhood success and long remembered. Nell had made another deal with Papa which resulted in Papa being the owner of Nell's prized doll buggy, her present from Santa the year before. She felt very secure this time, for she could not imagine that Papa could use or sell a doll buggy. Her distress in getting out of the deal with Baldy was already forgotten. Christmas was over, New Year's Day was the day after Christmas, so Nell thought. They had gone in the sleigh to Aunt Betsy's for New Year's Day dinner. That was a special treat.

Then disaster struck. Cousin Rick's house burned with everything in it. In a rural community there was no way for people to gather quickly to fight the furious blaze or salvage anything.

When Mama heard, she quickly washed and ironed Nell's best gingham dress and gathered a few things to send to the family. Little Alice was one year younger than Nell, but Mama was sure the dress would fit. She had nothing to fit a little boy.

Papa hitched up Jim and Maude to the sleigh and made a long tour of the neighborhood and far beyond asking donations of food, clothing, bedding, furniture, bag of potatoes, apples, money, anything to help this needy family. He returned with a sleigh piled high with contributions freely given! So the family was able to move into an empty lumberman's shanty that housed them comfortably quite a few years.

The winter was dragging on with deep snow and bitter cold. Before January was over everything was so dull. Mama was always busy, churning, sewing, knitting, darning socks. Nell was fascinated with the churning, but the winter task was more tedious. The cream was too cold or too thin to turn into butter quickly. Mama's churn was a stoneware jar, the lid had a round hole which allowed the wooden dasher to be moved up and down. The cream, about one gallon, was poured into the jar, the dasher placed in the cream, then the lid fitted over the dasher and Nell eagerly went to work. Sitting on the stool she raised the dasher just so high then down. Up and down, up and down, it was fun for a while. As the cream began to thicken it followed the dasher through the hole in the lid. Nell stuck her finger in the cream to get a lick. It wasn't very tasty, so she didn't do it often. But up and down continued on and on. Her arms got very tired but the butter or cream was stubborn. After fifteen minutes, no luck, after thirty minutes maybe she thought she could hear a splash. She looked at the dasher handle. There were small drops of butter and milk on the handle. The miracle had happened; cream turned to butter. A few more strokes and Mama took over. She gathered the butter into a large lump in the butter bowl and worked it with a butter ladle until all the milk was pressed out. Then it was rinsed with water and salt was added. The family's supply of fresh butter was prepared for the week. Nell got a drink of the fresh buttermilk. There would be buttermilk pancakes for breakfast and buttermilk to go with Johnny Cake for Sunday night supper.

Papa and the boys were working in the swamp getting out cedar posts, logs, and tanbark for the mill at the river.

The jolt came one morning when Papa said quietly, "You know little Alice and her brother lost all their Christmas presents in the fire. I think I will just give Alice the doll buggy for she would like it very much."

Nell was faced with a big problem. She couldn't ask Mama to plead for her. She knew she had made a big mistake. How could she defend her rash promise? She quietly left the table and tried to re-think her childish behavior. She decided to do nothing for the time being.

She thought, "Winter can't last forever. So I'll make a set of paper dolls and have them talk to each other." Mama had taught her how to fold paper and with the big shears cut out a doll with the skirt already on. The big shears were heavy and clumsy. She kept at it and made all sizes of dolls with many dresses and garments. It didn't matter that each doll figure had a fold right down the middle of it.

She kept her family of dolls in an empty shoe box. She was so busy that she didn't like to leave when Mama called, "Nell, I need an armload of wood."

One morning Nell got up with a sore throat, swollen eyes and itchy red spots. Mama took one look at her and said, "Young lady, you have Chickenpox. You must keep warm and don't scratch. I'll fix you a bed on the couch. First I'll give you a bath of baking soda in warm water that will ease the itching."

Nell spent the next few days in and out of bed. The strange thing was that all the children in the paper doll family had Chickenpox too!

The days were getting longer. Papa was talking about spring plowing and planting.

Mama was planting her vegetable seeds in boxes of soil in the kitchen. She would have nice sturdy plants to set out in the garden when the weather warmed up.

The hens were getting broody; soon there would be new baby chicks!

O joy! Spring was here once more. Nell was eager to enjoy the bright new world of outdoors again.

The New House

Each day was the same; each day was different. Nell was so taken with her own interests and wishes that she was an oyster all to herself.

After Christmas she thought the next day was New Year's Day. Before she knew it spring was here; beautiful, bountiful blooming spring!

The weather was getting much warmer. It seemed suddenly that Papa and the boys had been building a new house! It would be their very own house.

To get there the family had to walk by cutting crosslots, climb a wire fence, follow a narrow path through brushy tangle to a clearing. Then surprise, the new lumber skeleton of a house showed up in the midst of many black stumps and sawhorses among the litter of scattered boards!

Papa warned, "Nell, be careful, watch where you are going, don't climb, don't fall over loose boards." Papa called, "Nell, stay out of the way." Papa had a long slivery board that he was making smooth with a hand plane. What fascinated Nell was the long curly shavings that came from the plane and fell to the floor. Nell could play with these long clean-smelling curls. She could wrap herself in them, fill her arms full of them. When she was tired she went sound asleep in a huge heap of them. The first family member to sleep in the new house.

Anyway, the days seemed to drag. The trip back and forth to the new house grew tiresome. They carried a meager lunch and drinking water, for the new well was not dug yet. Touching the blackened stumps, then slapping mosquitoes on her face and arms, Nell was usually quite smeared up. When the boys got their faces all black and grimy, they boasted that it showed that they had been working hard. So Nell copied their boasting and felt much better.

When the roof was on the new house and the sides boarded up, then it was covered with black tar paper. The paper was held in place by nails sheathed in small, shiny, round tin washers to keep the paper from tearing. They followed in straight rows, right and left, up and down, making a neat pattern. Next, windows and two outside doors were put in place.

The family eagerly moved in. But the move was so gradual that Nell could not remember when it happened. She was fascinated by the new metal door knobs and the beautiful glass in the door. The glass was too high for her to see out unless she stood on a kitchen chair. That was what she did when she had to tend door as Danny brought in armfuls of wood every day. He would call out "open" then she would turn the knob, jump down, pull the chair away, then open the door for Danny and close it. She did this many times until both wood boxes were full. She was doing useful work and it made her feel important. But Danny would often pull her braid or put a wet gloved finger in her face. Then she would shout, "Stop it!" But she was ready to open the door next time.

There were no complete partitions in the downstairs so Nell could amuse herself running in and out between the studs while the grown-ups had to use the regular door openings. Her lively imagination could entertain her for some time. The stairway was a fascinating place to play partly because danger lurked there. The stairs were solidly built but were not enclosed. There were no risers. She felt quite secure and dared to climb high. If the small kittens fell through they only got scared, not hurt, and it was fun to see them scramble to safety. But if Nell's foot slipped through, she had a scraped slivery leg or maybe a bumped face. Seated she could bump, bump down the stairs, chanting "One, two, buckle my shoe. Three, four," etc.

Then one afternoon when Nell was outside playing, she noticed billows of dust rising down the narrow wagon track road toward the turnpike. She also heard a strange chug-chugging noise. She finally could see what looked like a buggy coming along fast. But she couldn't see any horses pulling it! Frightened, she ran into the house calling "Mama, Mama!"

Mama also had heard the strange noise. She ran outside, overwhelmed to recognize the visitors. She greeted Grandma Abbott and Uncle Charlie with happiness and surprise. She helped Grandma down and admired the horseless carriage. When Papa came from the fields, the excitement increased as the men went into details of the adventurous journey.

Someone suggested that they should give Nell a ride in the newfangled machine. Nell wasn't sure. She felt safer on the ground. Then the question was "Where to drive?" Not back down the bumpy wagon track, not in the yard full of black stumps. While the decision was being settled, Grandma got back up in the seat and Mama helped Nell up to sit between Grandma and Uncle Charlie.

The decision was made to make a couple of trips around the house. Nell was tense and shivery. The engine was chugging so loud and the seat was shaking. They started slowly but Papa was leading the way clearing away sawhorses, boards, pieces of two-by-fours. Nell didn't like all this excitement because her fears were for Papa. She kept shouting "Papa watch out! Don't run over Papa!"

Nell did not know that Uncle Charlie had his foot on the brake pedal and could stop readily enough to give Papa a chance to clear a bumpy path. By the time they made a once around the house, Nell had enough ride. She was crying and shaking until they set her safely on the ground. She always remembered the fright and embarrassment of her first automobile ride.

She was a quiet little girl at the supper table, but she was all ears as Papa, Mama and the boys listened with intense interest to the great adventure.

Grandma and Uncle Charlie started out from their home in Mulliken in southern Michigan for the trip north. Their auto was a new two cylinder Reo with shiny brass carriage lanterns for headlights (they didn't drive at night). The wheels were high with narrow tires.

There were no road maps or road signs. There were no paved roads or gas stations or motels. Sometimes there was a grocery store at four corners. They could buy crackers or cheese or pickled bologna. They spent one night at Aunt Eva's in Saginaw County. Then at Bay City they followed the Ole Tote Road which had been the supply route to the northern lumber camps. They heard there were no gas stations farther north so they filled an extra five gallon can of gasoline and carried it along and trusted to luck.

They were so happy and relieved to arrive safely at the backwoods refuge of the Abbotts. They had probably traveled at least 250 miles over dirt roads and unmapped trails. They were very tired, hot and dusty, so bedtime came early.

The next few days were spent visiting. News of all the families was exchanged. Then thought of home and journey brought the visit to an end.

After Grandma and Uncle Charlie left chug chugging for their home, the family took up their regular work again. The boys with planting and now they spent many hours hoeing and mowing. Mama had extra work. Besides baking bread three times a week, washing all the clothes by hand, she did lots of work in the garden. Her work was often halted because a neighbor or friend was sick. She always was called and promptly rushed to help in an emergency.

Nell was busy, new kittens, new baby chicks to care for and love. The boys in the fields needed a drink of fresh water. Nell with her chubby legs was the water carrier. When she got back to the house there was a good sized wet spot in the sand where the wooden water trough leaked. The wet sand was just right to make mud pies. Also she could pack the wet sand around and over her hot bare foot, then carefully pull her foot out and she had a rounded hut with a wide entrance. She kept on until she had a village of mud huts. Summer was such a delight; she enjoyed each carefree day.

Papa was always building a new house for somebody. It could be a distant neighbor or maybe Uncle Frank and Aunt Betsy.

A song that was sung in Sunday School and in rural school started out like this:

"Work, for the night is coming,
Work through the morning hours,
Work while the dew is sparkling,
Work mid springing flowers;
Work when the day grows brighter,
Work in the glowing sun;
Work for night is coming
When man's work is done."

It shows the thinking and life pattern of folks facing life's struggles in the early 1900s.

Night Alarm

THE FAMILY WAS USED TO A ROUTINE that kept everyone busy. Mama saw to it that meals were ready on time. She expected the family members to be ready to eat on time as usual. Snacking was not indulged in, except in an emergency.

In summertime, Papa usually was away on the job of building somebody's new house. If it was quite a distance away, he was gone from Sunday afternoon till Saturday. Alan was hired by farmers during weeks of harvest. The family unit now consisted of Mama, Danny and Nell. They managed the chores, the gardening and fence mending quite well, but emergencies did happen.

One night quite late, Mama wakened Danny, "I am so sick." Then she passed out. Danny was very scared but very much in charge. When he couldn't revive her, he called Grandma Easlick on the phone. She said, "Try to keep calm; I'll be right over." She lived nearly a mile away.

Nell was very frightened and felt so helpless. Danny said, "Get dressed, take the lantern and go meet Grandma Easlick."

Nell welcomed the chance to be useful. She did not think of what she was getting herself into. She took the smelly smoky lantern and started out bravely. She hadn't gone very far from the yard when she began to have doubts. Her imagination took over, *What if Mama is really, really sick? I wish Papa could be home.*

And the lantern she clung to did not show much light. The night was very dark and beyond the lantern's faint light, the shadows were blacker and more frightening. Nell was sure there were no bears in these bushes beside the road. She took the cows along here every day. She had heard no bear stories in the neighborhood in a long time. But she listened intently for any sound of movement. A bird awakened by the light fluttered among the branches and startled her. She wished Grandma Easlick would soon show up.

She only knew that she must keep going and could not turn back. Footsteps made no sound in the deep dust of the road. But snakes! How could she see a snake in the dark? (She did not know that snakes do not venture out at night.) The farther she went the more scared she became. She was almost to the corner. But there were no travelers out on this road either.

She had the whole black world to herself. There was no moon or stars, just deep blackness. The lantern was a comfort but it couldn't still the rapid beating of her heart. She should soon be able to see lights from Easlick's house. But people didn't keep lamps burning all night. What if she had to go into their yard and knock at the door? She wasn't sure that the dog would be friendly at night. She was really scared and nervous, but she could only keep on keeping on.

Then suddenly out of the darkness a voice called, "Is that you, Danny?" Joyfully Nell ran to Grandma Easlick, "It's me, Nell. Danny sent me with the lantern. Mama is very sick and we don't know what to do." Nell was ready to cry with relief.

Grandma said, "Well you were a brave girl to bring the lantern so we can hurry along faster."

Back home Mama had come to. Grandma Easlick stayed overnight. At about 5 A.M. she went along home to prepare breakfast for her hungry family.

Danny was bleary-eyed doing the morning chores. Nell slept in later in the morning and didn't remember breakfast.

Mama was much better but very weak, so stayed in bed most of the day. She was very proud of Danny and Nell. They had performed well in an emergency. She felt that she would be safe when Papa was away in the future.

A Happy Day

One hot August day Mama stood expectantly at the kitchen window looking south when she saw children stirring up a cloud of yellow dust rising above the bushes along the road. She called to Danny, "Oh Danny, take Nell down the lane and show her the big watermelon. Don't pick any, but thump some of the bigger ones to see if they are getting ripe."

Danny instantly became an excited loving brother.

"Come along Nell. Let's go and see how the watermelons are growing. Hurry, let's run."

Taking her by the hand, they started out past the barn and down the lane. Nell was unaware of what was causing all of Danny's antics. But she was happy to be getting so much of his caring attention instead of his usual teasing. She could see nothing exciting about the melon patch.

"Look Nell, here's a nice sized one. It isn't ready yet. Listen." Thump, thump as he snapped it with his finger, testing. "It doesn't sound ripe. But over here is a bigger one. Be careful don't step on the vines. What about this one?"

He kept up the chatter as he hopped here and there over the patch. Nell was losing interest, but was still enjoying his brotherly attention. She was beginning to wonder at his silly capers.

Finally, Danny gave up and said, "It's no use; they must grow some more before they turn ripe. Let's go back to the house."

A sleepy green frog leaped out from the tall grass into the dusty path. But Danny wasn't interested in teasing frogs today. He was so anxious to get back to the house.

Mama was on the porch. To slow them down she called: "Danny, on your way in bring an armload of wood for the woodbox!"

Danny was most obedient and generous, for he loaded Nell's arms first with smaller sticks. Then he picked up the bigger ones in his arms and led the way into the kitchen. He didn't even hold the screen door open for Nell. When it slammed shut, it caught her bare heel.

Nell yelled in pain and anger. With blood dripping across the floor, she dropped her wood into the woodbox beside the stove. Before she could sob out her complaint to Mama, Danny rudely shoved her through the door into the living room. Nell's screams stopped abruptly. Seated on chairs and couch around the room were her friends and cousins, eight or so girls and one boy gleefully calling, "Happy Birthday, Nell!"

She wished the floor would open and swallow her. Trying to dry her tears she ran across the room into the arms of the biggest girl, Becky, and hid her face.

Mama brought a pan of warm water to wash the nasty cut. Then with Cloverine salve and white bandage she skillfully wrapped it, and calm was restored.

Within a few minutes the games began. One of the favorite games was "I Spy" or "Hide The Thimble."

The group had to go into the kitchen while *it* placed the thimble somewhere in the room in plain sight. Then walking away, assuming an indifferent pose would call out "Butter, Beans, come to supper!" The group would enter and ask, "How high is the water?" *It* would respond gesturing height with his hand, but not turning his eye, "This high." The frantic search began. The first one to spot the thimble would turn and quickly call "I spy" but make no move to remove it until others also discovered it. The first child to spy became *it* for the next round.

Meantime, Mama seated herself in the rocking chair to rest a minute and enjoy the fun. *It* placed the thimble in plain sight on Mama's finger of the folded hands. The group really searched high and low and accused *it* of hiding it out of sight. Finally, without having to give up, someone made the discovery to the delight of the whole group.

Then the game changed to Riddles and on to "Queens Dido Died."

"How did she die?"

"Doing this." A gesture, scratching head or swinging foot, was repeated around the circle with a recitation of the preceding motion and an original additive.

Such fun and hilarity went on for a very short hour till Mama had Birthday Cake with real whipped cream and Chocolate pudding ready.

Nell's gifts were simple but well received; a Birthday postcard, a new hair ribbon, a stuffed pin cushion, a lace edged handkerchief. Nell was very happy.

When the children had to start home, Nell went with them a piece down the road. They had a long walk to go and chore time when they got home. At the line fence Nell turned back, waving hands and calls of goodbye sending her on her way.

Nell walked homeward with mixed feelings. She remembered her embarrassment at bawling before her friends. She was happy that they had come. She had a good time. It was fun to play games and forget the heat. She was puzzled how Mama managed to keep the surprise, make the cake and everything. Dear, dear Mama.

Nell could not believe that she had been so blind and foolish not to suspect anything.

That brought her thinking to Danny. She was mad at Danny. He had lured her to the melon patch, made her hurry when it was so hot, made her carry in wood, and worst of all, let the screen door slam on her heel.

Now she would get even. Her sore heel would hurt too much to allow her to bring in the overnight wood. Danny would have to fill the woodbox all by himself!

At the supper table Papa and Alan were given all the details of Nell's Happy Birthday Party.

When chores were done and Nell was cuddled in Papa's comforting arms, she was pouring out all her troubles into Papa's listening ears. Papa gently said, "Many days hold both happiness, anger, pain and tears, laughter and tears, sunshine and rain. But we don't see rainbows unless first we have rain. Tomorrow is a new day. We will look for many bright tomorrows."